THE
STINGER
WARS

JOSHUA GOEHMANN

Order this book online at www.trafford.com
or email orders@trafford.com

Most Trafford titles are also available at major online book retailers.

Printed in the United States of America.

ISBN: 978-1-4907-4543-5 (sc)
ISBN: 978-1-4907-4544-2 (hc)
ISBN: 978-1-4907-4545-9 (e)

Library of Congress Control Number: 2014915238

Trafford rev. 08/26/2014

 www.trafford.com
North America & international
toll-free: 1 888 232 4444 (USA & Canada)
fax: 812 355 4082

Alcane realms stories. The stinger wars. I'm Riken Shatter of the stinger race, which was brought to near extinction. I know you haven't heard of us because four races tried to erase us from history. This is the story of those times and what led up to where we are today. The stingers are a very vicious race, even by demon standards and even very hard warriors, and the stinger king wanted to control everything. The other demons noticed the rising threat and tried to stop the stingers to no avail, so they struck an uneasy alliance with devils. Still their losses were great, so the humans who were no strangers to stingers joined in on both sides with promises of power, riches, and whatever they desired. So groups such as the vampires and werewolves joined as well. Still stingers fought harder and recruited more humans, turning them into stingers. So the angels joined, and those alliances almost destroyed the stingers. But the alliance between those groups could never last. One group of stingers left, led by my ancestor Tehila.

The enemies turned on each other. The stingers fled to hide. They were thought to have died out, so their history was erased so no one could seek them out so that they would cease to exist. So stingers faded into myth now. Today, demon hunters believe that stingers are just stories to scare kids. But no, the stingers are real, and we will rise and no one will stop us this time. The stingers have survived, and we are getting stronger as you races sit and grow weak. When we attack, we will show no mercy.

CHAPTER 1

One hundred fifteen imps, twenty succubus wolf pack, ten demon arms, five dretches.

Stryke: Rogue Storm, one of the scouts of, a black stinger called shadow stingers a 5'8 220 some ibs pound stinger in his first form. What do you see?

Rogue Storm: Not much of a threat. The worst one is the balor, which seems to be twelve feet tall. The face resembles a horned wolf. I see a handful of imps, some succubus, dretches, and some demon arms. Not too bad.

Stryke: Has Rogue Shadow rejoined Kestix's group?

Rogue Storm: Well, he was heading back as well.

Kestix is a heavily muscled iron skin stinger, about seven-foot-four and four hundred pounds of pure muscle in his second form. He has two horns curved forward, two eyes that look like there are three pointed stars in them, a mouth full of sharp teeth, demon marks like tattoos all over his body, his ravenlike wings, and two spearlike tails—enough to intimidate anyone.

Kestix: Okay. So we will start the battle. I want your arrows to take out the dretches, succubus, and arms first and wait to regroup to take on the balor. Stryke's group will charge in as soon as our first volley hits the demons. Okay, take aim and fire!

The first volley of arrows hit, covering two demon arms and four succubi with arrows. They were dead before they hit the ground. Stryke's group attacks from behind, killing the five dretches right away. Stryke dispatched two—one by slicing its head in two and slamming his spiked shield into the head of the other and slashing its neck for good measure, while another dretch takes a mace to the head from an iron-skinned stinger and then broke the arm of another to be dispatched by a dagger through the eye.

The remaining dretch tried to flee and took an axe to the back of the head of the two arms, and the succubi engaged Stryke's group. Stryke cut one arm down the middle and sliced a succubus from shoulder to hip. Kestix's group charged to the other side of the camp, firing more arrows and getting more succubi and imps. This time, Kestix slashed with his scythe, catching three imps and impaling all three on the end and swung it so they flew into another imp whom Kestix just smashed with his boot. Stryke then noticed the balor coming toward his group, slashing at one of the iron skins and causing his armor to frost up and getting his whip around the neck of pure blood, setting him on fire, which means the balor has an ice sword and flame whip. The balor uses the whip to throw the pure blood who uses magic to put the fire out and uses the momentum of the throw to fly back around, launching an acid ball on the balor. Kestix's group finishes with their imps and succubi and started shooting arrows at the balor while some were hitting it with lightning bolts, fireballs, acid balls, and ice spikes.

Kestix slashes the back of the balor's knee with his scythe taking to one knee. Stryke rushes in with his sword shield bashing its hand and slashing the wrist with his sword, driving it halfway through the balor. He jerks its hand, pulling the sword from him and pulling Stryke to his knees in front of the balor. Rick jumps into Stryke to save him from the descending ice sword, getting Stryke out of the way but getting his foot cleaved into a spear thrower, launching his spear into the balor's left eye. While the balor grabs the spear and pulls it out, Kestix drives its scythe into the back of the balor's head and out the front, and an iron skin smashes his hammer into the side of his head for good measure.

Kestix: Storm Shadow, search the place. Medic, check Rick. General Stryke, you okay?

Stryke: (*groaning as he gets up*) Never better.

Shadow: Stryke, we found a portal.

Stryke: Where to?

Shadow: Human realm.

Stryke: We need to report this to Inferno. Kestix, keep your group on high alert. I'm going to inform the grand lord.

CHAPTER 2

Lord Inferno, the Wolf Pack has returned.

Inferno, the stingers' grand lord, is in his 4000s. A seven-footer, five-hundred-pound monster in second form who basically has enough horns to create a crown on his head, glowing red eyes that appear to be on fire, demon markings all over his body that appear to be smoken, with his ten-foot, six-hundred-pound flamberge at his side.

Inferno: Ah, bring them in. How'd the raid go, General?

Stryke: Quite well. Twenty stingers killed fifty demons, including a balor, and we've uncovered a portal to the human realm.

Inferno: Start using it immediately. Capture any human to be transformed into stingers.

Stinger Captain: Yes, my lord.

Acrid is a rot angel just dripping his rotting affliction everywhere he goes in his special armor.

Acrid: really were making more tainted bloods. I'd have just executed them all.

Inferno: You may be one of my most trusted allies, even for a rot angel, but this is why you're still only a colonel. We are going to take over many realms, and for that we need armies.

Acrid: You already have legions at your disposal. Do you need more?

Inferno: We are going to rule more than just the demon realms, Lone Wolf.

Lone Wolf is the stingers' best recon specialist. He's a shadow stinger—a black skinned version of a stinger.

Lone Wolf: Yes, my lord.

Inferno: I want you two to check where that portal exactly goes to.

Lone Wolf: It will be done.

Messenger: Ekolid I do not like giving messages to Garol.

An ekolid resembles the combinment of an ant, scorpion, and spider. He will not like the news.

Messenger: A camp has been wiped out.

Garol: By who?

Messenger: Looks to be a stinger raiding group.

Garol: Do you know how many are there?

Messenger: Looks like only ten.

Garol: Go and tell one of the balors to go and take some dretches and what he wants with and kill all of them.

CHAPTER 3

Lone Wolf: Is the portal ready?

Stryke: You sure you want to go?

Lone Wolf: I will not disobey orders from Inferno.

Stryke: We'll be here when you get back.

Lone Wolf steps through the portal and ends up on earth. In a forest to his right is a facility. Lone Wolf casts a transparency spell and gets to the gate and picks the lock. There are a lot of sentries here. And gets into the building. Lone Wolf thinks they are making robots and androids—a human made with robotic upgrades to outdo a regular human. Inferno would like this.

Inferno: Welcome back, Lone Wolf. What did you find?

Lone Wolf: It's a robot and android facility to upgrade humans. It's either a big threat to us or an advantage.

Inferno: I say attack the facility, capture the scientist, download all the files, and destroy it. Bring the scientist back and we'll use them to make robotic demons.

Lone Wolf: Who's going to assist with that?

Inferno: I'll send my three top groups: Nightmare Squad led by Acrid; the Death Squad led by the stinger hybrid, Raptor; and you will also meet up with Wolf Pack and inform them that they will be joining you.

Messenger: I've been watching the camp as you ordered, and the last you sent was slaughtered. Now there are more troops there, and some have gone through the portal. I think they are going to do what you are planning.

Garol: I want you to ready my group. If my underlings can't take care of this, I will do it myself.

Lone Wolf: I am to inform you that you guys will be helping in taking the facility.

Stryke: Who were the other two groups?

Lone Wolf: Those were the Nightmare Squad and Death Squad.

Kestix: But those are Inferno's legendary groups.

Lone Wolf: Yes, this is a high priority mission. We will be ready to attack in an hour. Nightmare Squad is in charge of protecting the building from enemies. Death Squad will try to clear all opposing targets. Our job is to take the scientist prisoners and to download all data and to set and arm that bomb. We will then return to the demon realm.

Acrid: I want you guys to take out the sentries quietly and then take their places.

Raptor: When we attack, kill whoever is in our way. That's our only order. Make sure Lone Wolf and Wolf Pack can get the scientist and data. Nightmare Squad One, in position. Nightmare Squad Two, in position. Nightmare Squad Three, set.

Nightmare Squad One fired their crossbows into the left side of watchtowers, littering the sentries full of arrows. Nightmare Squad Two used spells to quiet them and flew into the watchtowers and snapped or slit the throats of the guards there.

Acrid: Death Squad One or Two, do you see any more sentries?

Nightmare Squad One: Negative.

Nightmare Squad Two: All clear here.

Acrid: Okay, let's move. Okay, Death Squad, Wolf Pack outside is clear.

Raptor: Wait for our call before you come in, okay? Death Squad, split up. Death Squad One, take the roof. Death Squad Two, get the back, and my squad three takes the front.

Death Squad One leader: Burst the top floor room. Everyone down on the ground now.

The guards all lie facedown.

Death Squad One: Top floors seem like the barracks fit troops, and the scientists want them alive or executed.

Raptor: If they are scientists, Inferno wants them alive. Guards can be executed. Execute the guards in any way you want.

The stingers took out their enchanted syringes filled with their acid blood, put them into a vein, and injected it in the acid. Blood started burning the veins from the inside out and kept burning until it killed the heart and melted the body away—a painful way to die. Stinger blood expands when touching another liquid.

Death Squad One leader: Top floor secure.

Death Squad Two leader: Going in.

Raptor: Affirmative. Let's go. The first floor is empty. Well, here's some stairs going down.

Raptor and his group go down only to run into programmed and ready androids. The first androids shoot fire from their flame thrower and arms at the cramped stingers. Raptor goes demon form. two growing the two spearlike poison tails and two serpentlike heads and bodies from his back, thus releasing a small shock wave, destroying the two incoming androids. He readies his five-hundred-pound war hammer. Raptor sidesteps a sword swing from the android and smashes the right side of the android's face, but the android continued like it was nothing.

my right serpent head but into his shoulder and the other head grabbed his other arm and lifted him off the ground and stabbing his tails into his face. I know the poison won't do anything, but I can destroy him. Raptor looks back to the rest of the battle. The Death Squad is badly outnumbered and barely fighting them off. I need get to that control room. You three with me, I need get to that control room. The magic casting stinger was just using telekinesis to throw android aside, and the two iron-skinned ones were just smashing them out of the way, doing no real damage but clearing my way, and the magic user launched a fireball at the control room window, blowing molten glass into the unfortunate scientist on the other side.

Raptor jumped through the window and grabbed the badly injured scientist. Turn them off, and your death will be quick. If not, it will be painful and slow. That button there, I press it and the androids powers off. Raptor- uses telekinesis to slowly push the molten glass into his skull through his brain.

Scientist: You said it would be quick.

Raptor: I lied.

Lone Wolf: Is it ready?

Raptor: You just need to hack it.

Lone Wolf: Stryke, have your group set the bombs. I have the detonator.

Acrid: Guys, we have a problem.

Lone Wolf: What is it?

Looks like a small demon army led by an ekolid.

Lone Wolf: Get your spell casters down here. We can open a temporary portal to Inferno's palace. We may have to sacrifice some of your men to get out of here.

Acrid: They all knew that death was a possibility. Send about twenty of our iron skins up. The army will have trouble getting to us in the small stairway. They can hold them off.

Raptor: Casters, start creating the portal. It may take a bit magic. It is not as strong in the human realm, Acrid. The fight up there is already beginning. They can take a lot more than they number.

Caster: The portal is about ready.

As he says this, a deformed mix between a spider and scorpion makes it down.

Caster: Garol, you shall all die.

Raptor and another stinger tackle him infinite wall and start punching, kicking, kneeing, biting, and stinging each other. Raptor, go through now. Lone Wolf jumps through and activates the detonator, and the facility is leveled.

Inferno: Why have we so few members?

Lone Wolf: A small demon army attacked the camp, killed everyone there, and went after us at the facility.

Inferno: Did you get the data?

Lone Wolf: Yes.

Stryke: Do you even care that we almost died? About twenty-two of us are dead, including Raptor.

Inferno: Silence! Do not make me show you why I am the grand lord.

Stryke: Well, why don't you, my grand lord?

Before Stryke relived it, Inferno was five feet away, swinging his flamberge at Stryke's neck. Stryke rolls under and gets his shield up to block a swing from Inferno, but the attack had enough force to send him flying back into the wall ten feet away. Inferno charged in, and Stryke dodged to the right and barely missed a downward slash that would have cleaved him in half. Stryke shield bash, and Inferno grabs the side of the shield and throws it to the side and knees Stryke in the ribs, breaking a few, followed by a pummel strike to the head taking Stryke to his knees. Inferno sheathes his sword and punches Stryke in the nose shattering the bone there then breaking his jaw and continued to pummel Stryke until he was bloody and unconscious.

Inferno: Does anyone else want to question me?

No one answers.

Inferno: Give my scientist the data and have the prisoners turned into stingers and have them spell bound into loyalty and throw Stryke in his quarters.

Lone Wolf: Yes, my lord.

Lone Wolf: All of you will become stingers. We will inject you with two things: stinger blood and a potion to neutralize the effects of the acid. You will become a tainted blood and will swear a spell-bound loyalty to Inferno. If you break that vow, you will die a painful, slow, magic-induced death.

Kestix: Stryke, you're awake.

Stryke: Well, I think I was knocked out not asleep.

Kestix: Good to see he didn't knock the humor out of you, but what were you thinking? Talking back to him, he could have killed you.

Stryke: But he didn't. I don't know why, but I think we're more valuable than you think.

Kestix: Never do that again. He may kill you next time. He's done it before.

Garol: (*climbing his way out of the ruins*) *Did they think that would kill me? I will find out where they went and kill them, but I will die by myself. I'm going to need help. Gotta join a demon lord's army and explain what they did. Maybe a devil will work.*

CHAPTER 4

....

The King of Hell

Lucifer is a devil—more like the devil. He's the king of hell, and all demons follow him to the letter, no talking back. He looks like most devils. He has long raven black hair, pointed and curved round horns, pointed elfish style ears, pure white eyes, a pointed goatee, pure red skin, a tail that looks like an arrowhead on the end, sharpened nails like claws on each finger, batlike wings clearly visible, and hoofed feet like a horse. The only differences from the other evils is, he's three times the original size, clearly over twenty feet tall, easily six hundred pounds, and at his side, his giant three-tipped pitch fork always dripping blood. Just the look feels like it's stabbing into your soul, and the look of him makes you want to drop to your hands and knees and beg forgiveness.

Garol: King Lucifer, I need your help. These stingers need to die.

Lucifer: And what do I get out of this?

Garol: The surviving stingers will be your slaves.

Lucifer: I have enough slaves already.

Garol: What about their souls and will give you any souls that I gather from my day on.

Lucifer: Are you aware how many souls come through the gates of hell in a day?

Garol: This stinger challenges your very own throne.

Lucifer: Very well. I shall watch him and decide if he's a threat or not. Until then, you are a guest here.

Three months later.

Lucifer: Hmm, many demons have banded together to try to topple Inferno's growing empire but failed. Maybe they are a danger, and being a stinger demon, I can't wait for old age to take them. They are immortal. They can only be killed, and do you have any demons under you left?

Garol: A few.

Lucifer: Bring them. We may need them. What kind?

Garol: Fifteen balors left.

Lucifer: I will give you fifty of my devils. Since devils are superior to demons, you should be able to handle it.

Garol: But he has legions of demons. How will—

Lucifer: Let me finish. You will tell them you want to join, and so do your minions. They may be happy to get some devils, and when you're in the city, attack your escorts and start screaming how the stingers have angered Lucifer, the king of hell, and that we need to kill the stingers to repent—or you will face Lucifer's wrath with the devils. They will believe you, and with you so close to the palace, Inferno may come out himself and yell that whoever kills him will become my right hand.

Garol: You are brilliant! (*thinks to himself*) *Just need to play him to kill the stingers, then kill Lucifer myself.*

Lucifer: I'll send some scouts to watch leave me. The devils will be ready.

Garol: Yes, Lucifer.

Lucifer: And take this. If you are in trouble, you can use it to teleport out of there.

Inferno: Well, now my armies have grown quicker than I thought.

Acrid: I never thought we'd get this many.

Inferno gives him a dirty look.

Acrid: This fast.

Inferno: Never doubt the stingers' abilities.

Garol: Greetings, mighty stingers. We would like to join the stingers' army.

Stinger guard: And who are you?

Garol: A demon lord.

Stinger guard: Not too well known, but I heard of you.

Garol: I brought my army—fifty balors and fifty devils.

Stinger guard: (*surprised*) Devils. I'm impressed. Inferno will like to meet you personally.

Garol: Let's go.

Stinger guard captain: (*opens gate*) You lead them to the palace.

Stinger guard: Yes, Captain. (*leads them through the city*)

Garol thinks: Just as many demons as stingers here. We have the upper hand.

Stinger guard: And this is the—

Garol swings his sword at his neck, cleanly cleaving it off; and the balors circle Garol, protecting him and using magic to increase the volume of his voice yells: The stingers have angered Lucifer, and his devils are here to kill the stingers and all who have aligned with them. He will kill all of you unless you turn on the stingers and genocide their entire race. Whoever kills the leader, Inferno, will become his right-hand man.

All hell breaks loose as the demons and devils attack the stingers from multiple sides. Many stingers die, with little casualties to the demons and devils.

Acrid: Inferno, the demons are rebelling with the help of devils, and it looks like the instigator is surrounded by many balors.

Inferno: Get the Nightmare Squad, Death Squad, and Wolf Pack. We're going to take care of this.

Acrid: We're—

Inferno: I need to show the demons what happens when you go against me.

Acrid: Are you sure that's wise?

Inferno: (*yells*) Do not question me! Just move!

Inferno picks up his ten-foot Long flamberge from its spot beside his throne and sheathes it behind his back and moves straight for the door.

Acrid: Sir, we are fighting back and gaining ground but with losses.

Inferno: Open the gate.

Acrid: But, sir—

Inferno: (*yells*) Do not disobey me! Next time there will be punishment.

Acrid: Sorry, my lord. (*opens the gate*)

And before it's all open with surprising speed, Inferno bolts toward the balors, protecting Garol. Seeing Inferno's minor demons and the devils go at him, Inferno slices through three demons, and a devil down with one swing. He puts an imp into a succubus and slashes her throat. A demon arm goes at Inferno and is cut to three pieces, and two balors move to intercept Inferno. The first balor swings its ice sword at Inferno in an overhead slash, and Inferno's flamberge bursts into flames and parries the blow one handed, and the second swings his sword at Inferno's chest. Inferno steps back out of range and rushes in and pummel strikes the balor in the ribs, cracking one of the other swings at Inferno's head. Inferno goes under and slashes through the balor's knee.

The balor goes back and is down to one knee, and the second swings his flame whip at Inferno and Inferno blocks it with his arm and it wraps around his arm and nothing happened. There's a reason I'm named Inferno and he slashes the balor's arm of at the elbow and swings his new whip at the balor and connects with his eye, setting it on fire and distracting is Inferno then jams the sword through the balor's spine and through its heart the other recovering rushes Inferno.

Inferno wraps the whip around the balor's leg and pulls it. The balor yells in pain and fury as his leg burns and Inferno silences as overhead swings his flamberge, cutting the balor in half from head to stomach and then grabs its whip. A third balor goes from him and he sidesteps kicks out the knee, forcing the balor to his knees, and then inferno rips a wing right off and then a second and snaps the balor's neck one way then the other and rips the head off and throws it.

A fourth balor goes for Inferno and Inferno just slashes its stomach with his flamberge and as the intestines fall out, Inferno jams his hand into the cut and rips out half the intestines and shoves the balor away. A fifth balor foolishly goes at Inferno, and Inferno, getting bored with this, just slams his arm through the balor's ribs and rips out its heart and crushes the heart.

The balor steps back and starts to flee in different directions, leaving Garol and the devils outnumbered because the demons have stopped fighting after that display and a devil goes for Inferno not knowing he has two tails. It runs face first into its poison tip and the second strikes the devil at the throat the devil falls back thrashing in pain as the poison goes for its major organs and Inferno steps to fight Garol. Garol then changes four of its arm into scorpion pincers and two into scorpion stingers and lifts its giant war axe with the other two and smiles evilly at Inferno and swings its axe. Inferno jumps over it and swings his whip around Garol's arm, setting the arm on fire. Garol lets go of the axe, and it flies into the back of one of the devil's head and stabs at Inferno with both stingers.

Inferno jumps to the right and swings the whip around both of them, pulling them together and cuts both of them off with his flamberge. Garol steps back and swings his pincher at Inferno. Inferno swings the whip around it and lets go of the whip, leaving it to scorch Garol's arm. Garol takes it and throws it and goes for Inferno again. Inferno grabs the arm and breaks it before ripping the arm off and reversing it. It launches like a spear into Garol's stomach. Garol lunges for Inferno, and Inferno slashs Garol appears in front of Lucifer rolling in pain not doiling. Garol screams and tries to bite Inferno, and Inferno gets his flaming flamberge in Garol's mouth and pushes back, cutting through the cheeks and forcing Garol to a wall.

Inferno: This is a lesson to all demons, even with devils. I'm invincible.

And he launches a fireball down Garol's open mouth and into his throat, and then Garol disappears.

Stryke: What just happened? Did he disintegrate that demon?

Kestix: I have no idea, but we should move to bring these demons back for punishment.

Garol appears in front of Lucifer, doling in pain.

Lucifer: Ah, as much as I love seeing you in pain—how did the mission go?

Garol: (weakened scream of pain)

Lucifer: Sounds like your throat is too wrecked to speak. Guess I'll wait for the scouts.

Two hours later.

Lucifer: (*screams in rage*) What! All my devils are dead, and the stingers are still strong? They will pay for this!

Garol, still not able to speak, nods.

Lucifer: What? That's all you can do?

He walks up and punches Garol, breaking his nose and knocking him over. Garol makes a sound close to a grunt.

Lucifer: What? Can you not speak?

Garol says something that Lucifer doesn't understand.

Lucifer: You may never speak again.

Seeing the fear in Garol's eyes brings some pleasure to Lucifer.

Inferno: How many are dead?

Acrid: About a hundred demons—seventy-five stingers and fifty devils.

Inferno: Take the stingers' bodies and dead iron skin. Make an armor out of his skin and clubs out of his bones the other ones make magic resistant items and magical staffs out of there bones even in death you may serve me

CHAPTER 5

Raptor: Damn! It took me long enough to get out of that ruin. I almost got killed. Damn Inferno and his grand ideas. I will start my own life without the stingers army.

Lucifer: Well, this is perfect—your telling me that the stingers are even able to match about any devil, even with other demons with us. This will be a hard fight.

Garol, no longer able to speak, writes out his idea of recruiting humans.

For our cause, they may be weak, but they can be cannon fodder. And vampires and werewolves would be a great help.

Lucifer: Good idea. You may be able to redeem yourself.

Inferno: I didn't want to fight the devils just yet, but it looks like we may need to beat them into submission too.

Acrid: What would you like me to do?

Inferno: Ready an army. We need to be ready to attack and send the Wolf Pack on a recon mission off the devils' realms.

Acrid: It shall be done.

Scout: My lord.

Inferno: What is it?

Scout: There are demons in the human realm.

Inferno: And why does this concern me?

Scout: Spies report that they are trying to add humans to their ranks for the war against the stingers. And they have even employed the fallen angel, Ezekiel.

Ezekiel is an angel that was thrown out of heaven for the fact that he viciously kills and slaughters demons, devils, summoners, and worshipers of these creatures, and he even enjoyed doing that his evil side has changed his angelic appearance. His wings are no longer white; they have turned black. His voice is no longer enlightening to those who hear it.

Inferno: Well, this is becoming an even bigger war than I thought.

Client: We have a mission that you may find profitable.

Gabriel: And what might that mission be?

Client: Well, do you know anything about the stinger demons?

Gabriel: Yes, we know about that. An expensive hunt there. You know that, right?

Client: Yes. Money won't be a problem, and we have a lot to kill, including the king.

Gabriel: This is big job. You'll need to talk with Ezekiel.

Client: Where is he?

Gabriel: On a job. He'll be back tomorrow.

Client: I'll be back, then. Ezekiel thinks these are the summoners—five elves. Why do they summon demons? Oh well, they are scum for doing that.

Elf leader: Tonight we shall summon a high demon lord. Tonight we shall sacrifice one of you to him for the power that will be granted to us.

Ezekiel, using the shadows, creeps up behind one of the elves and killed it with his assassin blade by stabbing him in the back of the neck, killing him halfway through the windpipe.

Elf leader: Intruder! Kill him!

Now Ezekiel pulls out his short sword, keeping his assassin blades out. The first one pulled two short swords out and went at him with a feint from high left with one and going down low with the right. Ezekiel saw it coming and blocked the bottom shot and slashed his throat with the assassin blade and moved to the next one while the other elf died from his wounds. The next one came at him with one long sword, and the other tried firing arrows at Ezekiel.

He dodged the first couple of arrows and engaged the long sword wielder, parting the first slashes leading the shots higher and higher and then goes down low on the slash cutting off the bottom two legs and charging the bowman, dodging and blocking arrows and, when he got there, slashing the bow in two and stabbing the assassin blade between the two ribs and puncturing one of his lungs and then punching him in the eye and taking him from his feet and neutralizing him, and then Ezekiel then steps to the leader.

Elf leader: Why are you doing this?

Ezekiel: You are a demon summoner, and those abominations should stay in their own realm.

Elf leader: Our religion is our own. What do you care?

Ezekiel: A demon would kill you, no problem. And I'm an angel, and angels hate demons, and you will die. And then he stabs his assassin blade into the leader's chest and right into his heart, killing him instantly.

Gabriel: We have a big job.

Ezekiel: What's the job?

Gabriel: To kill stingers. The client will be here today.

Ezekiel: Okay.

Two hours later.

Gabriel: The client is here.

Ezekiel: Bring him in.

Client: I have a great deal for you.

Ezekiel: And what is the deal?

Client: We want stingers killed—every single one.

Ezekiel: I usually don't ask why, but why all of them?

Client: They wronged me and my friends.

Ezekiel: So you want them all dead?

Client: Yes.

Ezekiel: You know how hard stingers are to kill, so they are expensive.

Client: Yes. I will pay two thousand gold per stinger and twenty thousand gold on their king.

Ezekiel: That sounds fair. You have a deal. Where are they?

Client: They are located in the demon realm.

Ezekiel: Well, we may need the entire company to do this deal. Let everyone else know the new job we have.

Gabriel: Okay, I'll let everyone know that we have a new deal.

Ezekiel: Okay. We'll start our new job today. Get the sorcesors. We need them to get to work on opening the portal to the demon realms

CHAPTER 6

Ezekiel: Well, there's the stingers' main city. We need to stalk the groups that are heading out. We will attack them, and we'll need to find out everything we can about their king, and then we'll have some money to hire some more help and getting more weapons.

Inferno: Stryke, I need you to take the Wolf Pack to the human realm so we can get some of our alliances going. We need all the help we can get.

Stryke: Who am I going to talk to?

Inferno: The Vector—he's one of the main werewolves and one of their main leaders. We need to get them to help us.

Stryke: Okay, we'll leave right now.

Gabriel: Ezekiel, we have a group of stingers leaving the city right now.

Ezekiel: Okay. Wait until they are a good distance from the city. We will then set up an ambush.

Kestix: Where are we going to travel?

Stryke: We're going to the lake of blood. We'll open a portal there.

Ezekiel: Okay.

They are stopped when they started casting a spell.

Ezekiel: We'll attack. We may need to keep one or two alive for information.

Gabriel: How do we to set it up?

Ezekiel: We will set up three groups. We'll attack from the right and left and a group will attack from the end of the lake.

Gabriel: They're talking to some blood demons.

Ezekiel: Well, at least now we know there are blood demons. They won't take us by surprise.

Stryke: All we are doing is making a portal to travel to the human realm.

Blood demon: Okay. When you're down, send one back to let us know.

Stryke: Okay, we will.

Blood demon: Good. Don't need any of them accidentally sent to human realm.

Ezekiel: Okay. Are the three groups set up? Jake just got back, and all three groups are in place. Okay. When the first group starts launching spells and arrows, the other two will attack, and keep only two alive.

Gabriel: I'll let Jake know to tell the third group.

When the spell needs to be done, the demon hunters shoot their enchanted arrows. Their enchanted arrows can go through almost the best armors. The closest five get hit by a storm of arrows. The first five were dead before they hit the ground, and the two other groups attacked from both sides, killing some of the Wolf Pack members within a couple of seconds, and then it became a killing ground. The ground was being soaked in stingers humans and angels blood. Ezekiel draws his sword and engages the first stinger he sees. This stinger is about five-foot-ten with full body armor wielding a ten-foot great sword. This stinger does a good job at keeping Ezekiel at a distance, swinging this giant sword like it's nothing. So Ezekiel fake-trips forward, and the stinger goes for it.

Ezekiel pushes his hand on the flat of the blade to get him over the great sword, and rushing in, he swings hard enough to connect with the stinger's hand with enough force to break a normal man's hand, but this seemed to do almost nothing to this man. This stinger punches Ezekiel with enough force to send him several feet back. There seems to be a small opening at neck level with this stinger. The stinger swings at chest level. Ezekiel ducks under it and goes forward with the assassin blade going for the opening and gets it before the stinger could stop it. The blade right through opening and into the stinger's wind pipe. Gabriel was in a battle with a female stinger who wielded two short swords with very surprising speed.

Gabriel was having trouble keeping up and had a lot of small cuts and a deep gash across his forearm. and Gabriel knew that he couldn't beat her, so he did a suicide rush into her. She didn't expect it, so Gabriel was lucky enough to keep the swords from his throat and drove her into some incoming arrows and, with a final push, sent into the lake of blood. When she hit and went under, she didn't come back. Gabriel turned only to catch the handle of a scythe to his head, sending him back above the blood lake. And through his mind, it's over for me. He waited for an end that never came and realized that someone used telekinesis to send him toward the bowmen and safety. Ezekiel, seeing this scythe wielder, goes at him only to take a spiced shield bash on his arm and loses all feeling in that arm and is now defending against a new attacker with a shield.

Kestix sees a angel with two short swords sending Sarah to the blood lake, so he rushes forward and smashes the bottom of the scythe handle into his face, knocking him out and sending him into the lake, but then his body flies across the lake to the enemy bowmen. Stryke spots the legendary Ezekiel and slams his spiked shield bash into his arm. Ezekiel blocks the pierce, slapping the shot away and hilt, bashing Stryke on top of the head and taking him to his knees, and then Ezekiel gets blinding pain, and his right wing was on the ground. Kestix is taking arrows to lower back, and Stryke grabs Kestix and yells for his troops to retreat, and Gabriel does not pursue. He gets his wounded man and Ezekiel back to the human realm to heal up with about twelve out of twenty of the stinger group dead.

Inferno: I didn't think they'd be that dangerous. Maybe we should send out the Nightmare Squad. By the way, have you found a new leader for that group?

Leech no one sees leech outside his armor, only unlucky slaves or high-ranking members of Inferno's army. Leech is usually in his black spiked armor, but that's because he looks deformed due to a battle he had against Inferno. He had his armor melted to his skin and barely survived, so Inferno decided he would be a good member to his army, and he was right. And Leech's weapon is devastating, like a giant war axe with a hammer on one side and axe the other with a hook blade on the bottom.

Acrid: Yes, I've decided to put Leech in charge of that group.

Inferno: That's a good pick. You should send his group out to destroy Ezekiel's head quarters.

Acrid: Yes, sir.

CHAPTER 7

Leech: So you want me to go to the human realm and destroy a building and kill everyone there?

Acrid: It's a high-priority target.

Leech: Any information on who's in the building?

Acrid: A bunch of humans and angels.

Leech: Angels? Well, they may sate my hunger for a little longer. When do I start?

Acrid: As soon as possible.

Ezekiel: Well, that was somewhat successful. Let's restock, and we'll head out again. Gabriel, are you listening?

Gabriel: I think we're being watched. Let's go that way.

Ezekiel: Let's see who it is.

Gabriel: Me right you left.

Ezekiel: Sounds good.

Ezekiel: Stop right there. You're not human, you're a stinger—a spy.

Raptor: I'm not a spy. I'm a former member of Inferno's army but not anymore.

Ezekiel: What do you mean?

Raptor: Was left for dead and decided to take early retirement.

Ezekiel: Well, my spells don't detect that your lying. Well, be careful. You aren't really welcome out here. But hey, want a job? Part of the pay is, we'll bring you the supplies you need from town with the money you make from us.

Raptor: And what's the job?

Ezekiel: Since you wouldn't be welcome at headquarters, you will just be watching for trouble.

Raptor: Sounds good. You have a deal.

Ezekiel: By the way, what's your name?

Raptor: I'm Raptor, and you?

Ezekiel: I'm Ezekiel.

Raptor: (*surprised*) You're the fallen angel.

Ezekiel: That's me.

Leech: So that's our target. Thought it would be better defended. Oh well, time to have some fun. Let's go.

Raptor: Is that the Nightmare Squad? What are they doing? Oh god, no! Stop!

Leech: Raptor! Is that you? I thought you were dead.

Raptor: Far from it.

Leech: Well, you're just in time to help us remove a thorn from Inferno's side.

Raptor: And who would that be?

Leech: That building.

Raptor: No. Turn around and leave.

Leech: This is an order from Inferno himself. I'll kill you if I have to.

Raptor: I never did like you. Fine. Bring it, you deformed shell of a former man.

Leech: I'll enjoy feeding off your body.

Raptor pulls out his war hammer

Leech: Still using that weak hammer?

Raptor: We'll see how weak it is when I crush your skull with it.

Raptor rushes at Leech and swings the hammer. Leech blocks it with his weapon and does an upward slash at Raptor with the hook and gets a small cut on Raptor's stomach and swings the axe side at Raptor's head. Raptor ducks and slams the top of his hammer into Leech's ribs, knocking him back.

Leech: Should have kept your armor.

Leech swings his axe at knee level. Raptor jumps onto the weapon and runs up the weapon at Leech. Leech hits Raptor back with a wind attack and rushes with a swing and followed by a hook slash then an acid ball, which Raptor blocks, but the acid eats through the middle of his hammer.

Leech: Foolish Raptor. I was always the better fighter than you.

Raptor slams the acid covered side of his hammer into Leech's helmet and then releases a flash wave to blind everyone but himself temporarily and run for Ezekiel's building.

Raptor: I need to warn them.

Raptor bursts through the front door.

Receptionist: How may. . . Demon!

Two guards go for Raptor in different sides, but he dodges.

Raptor: Wait! I'm a friend.

Guard: Demons are not friends.

Ray: Stop! Ezekiel told me we have a new ally. What do you need?

Watchman: Sir, we have enemies coming.

Raptor: Shit! Not fast enough.

Ray: Who are they?

Raptor: The Nightmare Squad—second best group in Inferno's army. Fifty strong.

Ray: Shit! We're outnumbered by twenty men, ten angels, twenty humans, and a stinger against stinger troops. Shit!

Leech: You ten launch cannons into the front of the building and move forward when in range. Get ready for close-quarter combat.

Raptor: We need to retreat.

Ray: Get the women out the back.

Raptor: That takes half our people.

Ray: I won't let the innocent die.

Multiple cannons smashed through the wall, taking out two angels and five humans. One cannon smashed into an angel's face, killing him instantly. Another took one to the neck, breaking it instantly. One human took it to the arm and fell from the second-story walkway, dying from the fall. Others got hit in other places.

Raptor: Damn it!

Ray: Get them out of here, Raptor.

Raptor: Why me?

Ray: You know more about our enemies than I. Go!

Raptor leaves with the women. Leech and his troops get to the front wall.

Leech: Knock, knock. Ha-ha-ha.

Ray: Who are you?

Leech: No one you need to know.

He launches a thunderbolt at Ray. Ray sidesteps and pulls a large handgun and shoots Leech in the chest.

Leech: You need a stronger gun.

Ray thinks, What kind of armor is that? This is a .50-caliber handgun. Leech attacks Ray. Ray steps to the side and pulls a sickle out and strikes Leech's arm. Leech blocks and does an upward slash at heads chin. Ray backs up and slashes at Leech's throat. Leech lets it hit his armor and slams the spike of his armor into the forearm of Ray, impaling his arm and driving Ray to one knee, and he swings the hammer end at Ray. Ray rolls narrowly, missing the killing blow. Ray gets back to his feet and goes for a couple quick strikes on Leech. Leech lets them all hit and swings the hook up, opening a large gash up Ray's stomach.

Leech: You will never beat me. Surrender now and you may live.

Ray answers with a sickle strike at the head of Leech. Leech grabs the blade of the sickle and disarms Ray, breaking his arm in the process. By this time, all of Ray's allies are dead or gone with Raptor.

Leech: Tie him up. Inferno will like a word with you.

CHAPTER 8

Desperate Rescue

Raptor: Damn it! I'm going to try to go save Ray.

Rena: Well, if you go, I'm coming. We have alliances with the assassins and fighters' guild. We can get some help from those places.

Raptor: Okay, but we need to hurry. We don't have too much time. If they make it back, we won't have a chance to save them.

Rena: Okay, lets go.

Leech: Well, I think that Inferno will have quite some fun torturing information out of you.

Rena: Okay, Raptor, I got us about twenty fighters, six assassins, and five monks. You ready for this?

Raptor: Yes.

Rena: Asking have a plan.

Raptor: Not really.

Rena: We should set up an ambush and attack from both sides.

Raptor: Sounds good.

Leech: Keep moving, angel.

And suddenly, Nightmare Squad is attacked from both sides. Ray roundhouse-kicks Leech, stumbling him away, and Ray runs into the chaos and bumps into Raptor.

Raptor: (*cuts Ray's bonds and hands him two large daggers*) Let's kill this fucker.

Two monks are fighting Leech but doing no real damage. It sounds like some of Leech's bones break with each hit, but he isn't slowing at all. One monk hits Leech in the side of the head hard enough to take his helmet off to see a disfigured face and surprises the monk that he isn't a stinger and that distraction was all Leech needed to do an upward slash with the hook cutting the monks face in half and the slamming the hammer into the monk's neck, breaking it for good measure.

The other monk does an open palm strike to Leech's face, breaking Leech's nose, but Leech grabs the monk's arm before he gets away and knees the monk in the gut and slams the axe part into the monk's head, cutting it in half. Two more monks attack Leech, and he swings at both of them and rolls away. The other ducks under and goes in only to get elbowed in his face, taking him off his feet. Leech drives the hooked blade straight down through the monk's heart. The other hits him, turning Leech into another hit and swings at the new opponent who dodges. Leech does a backhand at the other who just rolls under to his friend, and they start running, and Leech pursues them.

The two monks roll forward, which was the signal for Raptor to swing his axe out at Leech, connecting right in his chest plate, cracking it and knocking the air out of Leech. The two monks do a double punch to the same place, widening the crack, and Rena jumps out and shoots him in the same place with a shotgun, and the armor is now falling apart in that one place. Raptor does another shot, but Leech blocks this one and gets shot in the arm and hit in the back of the head, so Raptor hits him again, The armor in that one place is gone, and Leech blasts a dark ball at Rena that explodes on impact.

Raptor: What? How can you use dark stinger magic that increases your aging?

Leech: Just because I'm not a stinger doesn't mean I'm not immortal.

And then two knives slams right into where the opening is.

Ray: Hit him where the knives are.

Raptor slams the war hammer into the knives, driving the knives deeper into Leech's chest, piercing his heart. Leech lets out a horrible scream and explodes into a ball of light instantly, blinding everyone close, and where he was stands a very powerful dark war hammer.

Raptor: That weapon . . . Its power is incredible! We could use that to beat Inferno.

Raptor grabs the war hammer, and there's another flash of light. When everyone regained their senses, Raptor is on his knees with what appears to be a part of Leech's armor around Raptor's arm, and Raptor is trying to tear it off with genuine fear in his eyes. Only Raptor can hear Leech. This is why I've survived so many battles. When I'm almost beaten, I take the form of a weapon that one of my opponents wield, and they usually thinks it's a powerful weapon. I crush their mind and take their body, and it looks like you're next.

Raptor: (*yells*) No! I will not die here!

Ray: Raptor! He grabs renas sword and rushes at Raptor, cutting his arm off and severing the link between Raptor and Leech. Leech appears in front of them again.

Leech: Die!

He readies a dark demon blast only to take a couple shurikens to the face, neck, and midsection. He blasts the trees and then shields himself from more.

Lone Wolf: Didn't think that was Raptor, but the way he fights proves it. I may need to help the Nightmare Squad out. What's that? Another group? Fuck! Must be Ezekiel's group.

Ezekiel: Looks like a battle is going on down there. You two scout it out to see what's going on.

Scouts: Okay.

Lone Wolf: Better intercept those two.

Scout one: What do you think is going on?

Scout two: No idea.

Lone Wolf: Greetings, elves.

There are two slender elves—one blond and one black-haired with swords with each of them.

Both: (*shouting at the same time*) Stinger!

Both blades are out one with flames on it, and another with a glow to it.

Lone Wolf: Hmm. A flame- and lightning-enchanted weapons this may be entertaining Lone Wolf steps is staging and his two poisoned daggers in his hands almost instantly as the two elves charge. Lone Wolf dodges the first one and sidesteps the second, cutting across the one he decided to call Lightning Blade's Stomach. He turns back to face the two, and then the one he calls Flame Blade comes in. Lone Wolf, using magic, blows out one of his legs, causing him to stumble forward. Lone Wolf goes for his throat. Flame Blade hits the dagger, causing it to narrowly miss its mark instead of just getting a cut across the side if his throat.

Lone Wolf turns back to Lightning Blade and begins dodging and stepping in a stabing Lightning Blade within the first thirty seconds. Lightning Blade has a dozen small cuts, and about six are near fatal. Then Lone Wolf blows him back with a wind blast to fight Flame Blade again after parrying the first hit. Lone Wolf drops one knife and grabs a little ball from his pocket and closes his eyes as he throws it at the ground, and it explodes into blinding light. And before flame blade recovers, Lone Wolf slashes his throat. He turns to look at Lightning Blade who is barely on his feet and throws his dagger into Lightning Blade's eye and has his other in his hand instantly and plunges right through his ribs into his heart. Lone Wolf rips the dagger to the side, slashing a lung just for the hell of it.

Lone Wolf: These are good swords. They'll make me a good price back in town.

Ray: Wh-why aren't you dead?

Leech: I'm not easily defeated.

Leech goes for a killing blow on Ray, but Rena blocks the shot, but it was strong enough to throw her ten feet back.

Leech: Don't interfere.

Ray stabs his dagger into Leech's chest. Leech just backhands Ray and lifts his blade for the final blow to Raptor. And before Leech does that, Leech gets hit with a lightning bolt, sending him flying back. Then a female Mage rushes forward.

Ray: Riva . . . Ezekiel's daughter.

Riva: (*smiles to Ray*) Get this injured guy out of here. I'll call for the retreat.

After she says that, she jumps to the side as Leech tries to cleave Riva in half and fireballs Leech on the right side if his face. Leech tries to hit Riva with a dark demon blast and continues shooting it. Riva stops it with a continued stream of ice, but she can tell this thing is stronger than her. Leech takes an arrow to the back of the neck, stopping his attack and barely gets a barrier up to stop it. Riva, using magic to amplify her voice, orders a retreat. The remaining fighters, monks, and assassins pull back and get away from them.

Stinger: Leech, should we follow?

Leech: No. We are to destroy the building. We should return and let inferno know about our partly successful mission and Raptor's betrayal.

Ezekiel: Whatever they are, they're coming this way. Hide! We are low on arrows, and we have wounded. Don't want to end up in a battle over our heads.

The group passes.

Gabriel: Are those stingers?

Ezekiel: Oh no! Please no. We need to get to the base.

Gabriel: Where are those scouts?

Angel scout: Ezekiel, the eleven scouts were found dead.

Ezekiel: This is not going well.

They arrive in sight of their base. Seeing it reduced to nothing but a ruin brought Ezekiel close to crying.

Ezekiel: How many of my friends were killed today?

He notices the group in front of the ruins.

Ezekiel: Let's see if we can help the wounded.

Riva: Father!

Ezekiel: Riva!

They embrace in a hug.

Ezekiel: What are you doing here?

Riva: I was helping to save Ray.

Ezekiel: Ray is still alive?

Riva: Thanks to me, some monks, fighters, assassins, and—surprisingly—a stinger.

Ezekiel: Where's Ray?

Riva: Near the end, trying to help Raptor with his wound.

Ezekiel: Ray, you're still alive!

Ray: Thanks to the quick thinking of Raptor and your wife and then help from your daughter.

Ezekiel: You okay, Raptor?

Raptor: I lost my arm, but I'll get better.

Ezekiel: So where's my wife, Rena?

Ray: I'm sorry, but she got hit by one of monsters' dark blasts. She's dead.

Ezekiel: What? She's dead . . .

Ray: I'm sorry

Ezekiel: I'm going to fucking kill that creature! I'm going to kill every one of them.

Ray: Wait! We need to organize and get more help.

Raptor: I know a secret way into Inferno's place. I'm sure we'll find Leech there. But we need to get organized.

Riva: Father, have you seen Mother?

Ezekiel: I'm sorry. I just found out she was killed today at that battle.

Riva: What?

Ezekiel: I'm sorry.

Riva falls to her knees, speechless, and begins crying. Raptor couldn't even look at her.

Inferno: So Raptor's a deserter? Hmm. Put a bounty on his head.

Leech enters the room.

Leech: Inferno, Raptor's still alive

Inferno: Yes. Wolf has just informed me of that. And why didn't you kill him?

Leech: There were too many enemies, but we destroyed Ezekiel's headquarters, and I took one of Raptors arms.

Inferno: So you succeeded at the original mission. Where's Ezekiel's head?

Leech: He wasn't there.

Inferno: Well, there's your next job—hunt him down.

Leech: Yes, my lord.

CHAPTER 9

Scientist: Can we see inferno?

Guard: You may enter.

Scientist: Inferno.

Inferno: Yes.

Scientist: We have found a way to neutralize a stinger's blood in a section of the body. We can turn them into some kind of cyber soldiers.

Inferno: Inform Leech of this, and tell him to come to this room.

Acrid: Yes, sir.

Leech: You called?

Inferno: Yes. I have a gift to help you kill Ezekiel.

Leech: And what would that be?

Inferno calls his guards in, and a black-haired animal comes with them.

Leech: What is this.

Inferno: It's a stinger nexus. Its name is Midnight. Call to darkness and it will come.

Leech: Come to me, Midnight.

A black-and-white striped tigerlike animal appears. It has four eyes; sharpened teeth from one side of the head to the other, looking like it's smiling spikes across its back; is about five feet long and two-hundred forty pounds; has three big talons on all feet; and has a tail that spikes into two and ends with a hook-shaped stinger on the end of both.

Leech: What the hell is this?

Inferno: It's called a nexus. I thought, with your weird version on pleasure, you'd find this a majestic beast.

Leech: I don't care what it looks like. It's if it can kill that matters.

Inferno: Well, we have a couple angel prisoners if you want to see it in action.

Leech: That would be good.

Midnight enters the arena, and an angel with twin scimitars enters the arena. The two walk to face each other. Midnight does not hesitate in attacking the angel. Slicing three big gouges across the angel's thigh, he hits one knee. Midnight jumps by, and two stingers hit the angel in the arm, numbing his left arm completely. Midnight jumps back over him, biting down on his head and breaking his neck.

Leech: This thing may just be worth it.

Inferno: Just tell it what to do and it will listen.

Leech: So it's completely loyal to its master.

Inferno: Yes.

Inferno: Contact Rickter. I would like to see him.

Acrid: What? I thought that Leech was after Ezekiel.

Inferno: He is. Rickter will go after Raptor.

Two days later, Rickter—a dark elf with white shoulder length hair; more muscled than most elves; dressed in jeans, shoes, a shirt, a weighted jacket, a cowboylike hat with enchanted bracelets, and a necklace; with a long sword—was at his side and his sentient chain at his side that he can lengthen at will and make it weigh more or less. It's sadistic and talks to him, and any blood on the chain strengthens him.

Rickter: You called for me, Lord Inferno?

Inferno: Yes. I have a job for you. You remember Raptor, right?

Rickter: Of course.

Inferno: He has betrayed us, and I want him dead. That is your job

Rickter: A stinger. Big shot.

Inferno: The pay will be pretty good. I'll promise you that.

Rickter: You always come through. I'll take the job.

Inferno: Good.

Acrid: So the dark elf hunts Raptor. Do you think he'll be able to beat one like Raptor?

Inferno: Raptor is at a disadvantage. He lost an arm, so he may need to use a different weapon now. But I have another idea. What's the town where Raptor was last spotted?

Acrid: It's called Carville.

Inferno: How many people live in that town?

Acrid: It's a small town with less that a thousand people.

Inferno: Does it have a military base?

Acrid: No. But it has a majority of demon hunters due to Ezekiel's demon-hunting business. But some of his best men are dead now.

Inferno: Get your Death Squad, Leech's Nightmare Squad, Stryke's Wolf Pack, and a thousand warriors. And get my death car ready. Tomorrow, I will join in the battle.

Acrid: Are you sure?

Inferno: What? You think that I would sit back and miss out in the fun?

Acrid: Understood.

Tempest: Are you sure you want to, honey?

Inferno: Yes. Tomorrow, even the humans will know the name Inferno Shatter, king of the demons and stingers.

Tempest: You will cause fear in the hearts of everyone.

Inferno: Yes. But for now, let's enjoy the night. I may not be back for a while.

Lone Wolf: Well, looks like they are oblivious to the danger. They are settling down for the night.

Inferno: Foolish humans, thinking they are safe. They will not soon forget this night. How far is the next town?

Lone Wolf: About ten miles.

Inferno: Good. None will survive. Acrid, Leech, Stryke, are you ready for a slaughter?

The three: Yes.

Inferno: Get ready, then.

Stryke: I hate him.

Kestix: Maybe we will get the chance to kill him.

Stryke: May take the entire Wolf Pack to do that.

Kestix: It's possible, and I'm with you. Remember that.

Stryke: Thanks. Let's get ready.

Inferno is starting the charge. The army that Inferno had already charged at the town with cannon wielders and spell casters launching cannons and spells on the city, demolishing the first buildings and killing close to a hundred people before the army even reached the city. And the some of Ezekiel's men were ready, along with some assassins, monks, and fighters, but they could not stand against the dark wave of stinger warriors slaughtering anyone in their way.

Ezekiel: No. What's going on.

Gabriel: The stingers are in the human realm, but we have also spotted Leech with some other big shots and an unidentified stinger with authority over Leech.

Ezekiel: That must be the stinger king, Inferno. Get Ray and Reva. We may need their help. If he dies, the war may end.

Gabriel: We may finally end this.

Ezekiel: No. You and Raptor need to get everyone out of here. The women and children need to be saved.

Gabriel: Yes, sir.

Ray: So how do we get to him?

Ezekiel: We will fly in with our troops and focus on main attacks on Inferno, followed by Leech, and then any stinger close. We want him dead.

Reva: Sounds like a suicide mission.

Ezekiel: Kind of is.

Reva: Well, we'll join Mother soon and send Inferno to hell in the process. I accept death. Ezekiel, let's go.

Acrid: Take out that group in the air.

Solider: Yes, sir.

And he was silenced by a bunch of arrows and bullets pretty much shredding him. And land near Acrid, Acrid launches some small bolts from his crossbow into the group, dropping two humans right away. An angel with a sword and dagger swings at him. Acrid ducks and brings his sword out of his gaulent, almost slicing Ray's throat. Ray's sword connects with Acrid's hand, but the armor protected him against the shot. Acrid launches a bolt into Ray's stomach, causing some pain but hitting no major organs.

Gabriel has his two short swords out and is rushing at the supposed king of the stingers but is stopped by a giant axe swing at his head. Gabriel rolls under only to turn back with a hammer coming at him. Gabriel ducks at this too. Leech goes for a quick slash with his hook blade. Gabriel steps back, avoiding that shot too. Reva, seeing the evil creature that killed her mother, launches a thunderbolt into the creature, knocking him off his feet and sending him about ten feet back.

Reva: Get Inferno. I have this one.

She then launches a fireball at Leech and hits him right in the face, exploding on contact. Leech responds with a stinger blast at Reva. She blocks it with a ward, but the explosion makes her take a step back, and Leech was already rushing through the smoke after her. Reva uses telekinesis to throwing Leech into a tree with enough force to break the tree, nearly missing being cut in half. Gabriel runs to take on Inferno. Gabriel swings his sword at Inferno's neck. Inferno blocks it with his ten-foot flamberge, and then flames appear across the flamberge.

Inferno goes for a slash at Gabriel's legs. Gabriel jumps over and slashes at Inferno's exposed hand. Inferno lets go of the sword, then launches a fireball at Gabriel's face. Gabriel does a backward roll to avoid it, giving Inferno the time he needs to get his flamberge back. Ezekiel sees Gabriel battling the one they think is Inferno, then goes for a stab into the back of his neck with his assassin blade. Inferno drops below it, then elbows Ezekiel in the gut, then slams Ezekiel's face into his knee with enough force to break Ezekiel's nose. Gabriel goes in with a slash with the dagger to the neck and sword slash to the knee. Inferno jumps against the sword and grabs Gabriel's wrist and breaks it, then he pummel strikes Gabriel in the right eye, breaking his eye socket.

Ezekiel feints up high on Inferno and then goes low. Inferno parries, then brings Ezekiel's blade into the ground, then pulls Ezekiel forward and rips one of Ezekiel's wings with the bone right out of his back. Gabriel is back on Inferno with one arm hanging limply at his side. Inferno sheathes his sword.

Inferno: This will make it more entertaining.

Gabriel slashes but misses. Inferno grabs his arm, twists it behind Gabriel's back, hits Gabriel in the back of the head, then puts his back to Gabriel and pulls him over, sending face first to the ground. He then stomps into the back of Gabriel's head, knocking him out. Ezekiel slashes his assassin blade across Inferno's hamstring, taking him to one knee and tries to follow up. Inferno punches with enough force to shatter Ezekiel's right knee cap, then drives Ezekiel into the ground and rips out another wing.

Inferno: You should join us. You're seen as an abomination to your kind. They even threw you out of that realm. The stingers would gladly accept you.

Ezekiel replies with twisting out and trying to stab his assassin blade into Inferno's eye. Inferno pulls Ezekiel up, punches him in the stomach, knees him in the side of the head, then takes his flamberge out, and flames the flat of the blade against Ezekiel's head, drawing little blood, then drives it up, taking Ezekiel's ear off.

Ray is still fighting Acrid, trying to keep his rot blades from hitting him. Ray parries one gaulent blade with his dagger and feints high and then goes midsection. Acrid blocks and spits a rotting saliva on Ray's short sword, rusting it through pretty quickly, leaving Ray to fight with a broken short sword and a dagger. Acrid tries using the same move, going for Ray's face. Ray ducks and stabs his dagger toward Acrid's head, barely missing but drawing a little blood, which starts rusting the edge off. Acrid fires a rot bolt from his wrist crossbow, getting Ray in the wrist and rotting his wrist from the inside out.

Inferno walks behind Ray and stabs his poisonous stinger tail. Ray looks down to his chest and sees the stinger coming out of his chest. Inferno uses his tail to throw Ray away from him. Ray was dead before he landed.

Inferno: Leech, don't kill her.

Leech angles his axe to barely miss Reva's head and kicks her in the face to knock her out.

Leech: Why?

Inferno: I'm pretty sure you would like another plaything, especially one that looks like her.

Gabriel saw his friend Ray die. He sees Ezekiel moving a little, and Reva, not far from him, is probably gonna be killed.

I can maybe save Ezekiel but not Reva, Gabriel thinks. *We have given the refugees time to get to the next town. We need to join them.*

Gabriel pulls out a horn and blows it, and the remaining defenders try to get out of there. Gabriel uses a spell to create a bright flash to blind all close enemies and gets Ezekiel. He then tries to fly away and is met by a stinger in the air. Gabriel pulls a small knife, stabs the stinger in the eye, and puts a bullet from his pistol in its head, then flies to the town.

Inferno: Let them go.

Then holds up both hands, creating a giant fire ball, then launches it into the running refugees. The ones unlucky enough to not be vaporized instantly were in intense pain because their skin was melting off their bones.

City Captain: Just saw a giant fireball kill about half the refugees—women, children, elders. Inferno doesn't care who it was.

Inferno: They have nowhere to go. Let that serve as a message. Let them think of it. With that in their minds, they will have to surrender.

CHAPTER 10

Lone Wolf: Got a message from Rickter.

Inferno: And that is?

Lone Wolf: He says no to attack the city.

Inferno: And why not?

Lone Wolf: He's gonna sneak in to try to kill Raptor.

Inferno: That will really help us. Okay, then. I'll wait.

Rickter thinks, *Surprising. No one guards the sewer gates, and no one sees me coming out of the manhole. Shouldn't be hard to find Raptor.*

Raptor: So they have fallen.

Gabriel: Most of us did, but still the refugees made it.

Raptor: You angels and humans are so foolish, risking your lives for people who can't fight.

Gabriel: It's different here than the demon realm.

Raptor: I can tell.

Rickter thinks, *So that's Raptor. One arm? Oh, may not be as fun anymore. Oh well, maybe I'll torture a stinger. That will be fun.*

Rickter stealthily follows Raptor to the refugee camp and watches him take a tent. It's a big tent, and he easily slips in.

Raptor: Wasn't sure who was following me, but now I see Rickter. Did you not know that we have spells that help us see stuff like that? Shadows didn't help you this time.

Rickter: Oh no. But now I get the fun of killing you in open battle.

Vengeance: Let's make him beg for his life.

Rickter: Sounds like fun.

Raptor: You won't get that pleasure out of me.

Rickter: With one arm, you can't wield your normal hammer.

Raptor pulls out a smaller hammer and goes stinger form with his two spearlike tails growing and two serpentlike bodies from his back. Rickter swings the chain at leg level to try to wrap Raptor's legs up. Raptor just jumps over and rushed forward with a strong swing of his hammer. Rickter ducks and comes up with a pierce going for the armpit of Raptor. Raptor's serpent's head bites ahold of the sword and drives it out of the way. Raptor knees Rickter in the nose and hears it break under the force, sending Rickter in a backward roll; and Rickter comes out swinging his chain up, staking in around one of Raptor's swinging and yanking it down and goes for a slash at Raptor's chest.

Raptor hits the sword to the side with a swing of his hammer and head-butts Rickter in the chest. Rickter is able to take that length in his chain and gets it to go around Raptor's neck and cartwheels out of range and increases the weight of the chain and tightens it. One of Raptor's serpent's head and tail are being used to lessen the pressure on his neck, and the other two try to get it off his left wing, and Raptor decides to fly into the tent's roof and keep going, ripping through the top of the tent and taking Rickter with him. Rickter shortens the chain, bringing him up to Raptor and pulls out his bone dagger and starts stabbing Raptor repeatedly in the chest and stomach.

Rickter: Today you will die.

Raptor: You'll die from the fall.

Rickter: Not if Vengeance and I get ahold of something.

Raptor slams his hammer into Rickter's knife arm and breaks it, sending his knife hurtling back to the ground. Rickter head-butts Raptor, disorienting Raptor who then replies with swinging his hammer at Rickter's head. Rickter moves his head back, and the hammer hits his already broken nose, breaking it in a second place and bites into Raptor's arm not drawing blood because Raptor's an iron skin and starts kneeing Raptor. Raptor replies by biting Rickter's head and pulling some of his hair and skin out and getting the chain of his wing, and the serpent head-bites Rickter's stomach and easily throws Rickter a couple feet away, getting his grip off the chain, and then tosses the chain in the opposite direction. He then hits Raptor in the back, sending him forward. Then a chick looking like fourteen appears in front of him with a green shine to her, covered in what appears to be green clothes. She hits him in the jaw, sending Raptor back.

Raptor: Who are you?

Emerald: I'm Emerald.

Raptor: Why are you attacking me?

Emerald: I can't let you kill my master, can I?

Then he puts both hands in the air, then pulls both hands down. It suddenly gets hot, and Raptor is hit with a lot of force, sending him back to the ground and smashing him through a building into the ground and then exploding and disintegrating him. Emerald uses her meteor spell to hit Raptor with a meteor, sending him down and flies to catch Rickter, then get his chain, Vengeance.

Emerald: Sorry for being late, master.

Rickter: (*says slowly*) Is he dead?

Emerald: I believe so.

Rickter: Let's get our pay.

Acrid: Aww, Emerald, nice to see you. What can I help you with?

Emerald: Rickter is out of the city.

Acrid: So Raptor's dead.

Emerald: Yes.

Acrid: Here's your payment. Stay in touch. We can use Rickter again.

Inferno: So he did kill Raptor? Surprised he survived though, and still don't know why he hangs out with that thing.

Acrid: It's familiar. It's a different kind of familiar for it's linked to his soul.

Inferno: Whatever. Get your rot arrows ready. Today the town will fall, and to show the stingers why we aligned with your species, the stingers will stay back and watch.

Acrid: As you wish.

Mayor Tindell: We can't stay here.

Guard Captain: We have a sewer that leads to the next city

Tindell: But that leads through the territory that Vector took for werewolves, and they won't be too happy with us being down there.

Guard Captain: We may have stuff to trade, or afterward we may allow them a place in the city.

Tindell: Let's try. Send some of your guards first so we may find out.

CHAPTER 11

Inferno: Go ahead, Acrid.

Tempest: Don't worry, honey. We will both make it alive. I hope so.

Acrid and the rot angels fly to the city and start launching their rot angels at the wall. Anyone they hit will start rotting from the arrow. The defenders try shooting back, hitting some of the rot angels but not doing as much damage. Tempest lands on the wall and pulls her rot lance off her back and slams the point into the and closes the guard's chest, breaking ribs and hitting some organs that instantly die and starts to rot away and spins around to slam into the side of another guard's head, sending to fall to his death while his face rots away.

Acrid, with some of his personal guards, lands in the refugee camp and starts killing anyone close. Acrid was looking for Gabriel and was launching rot bolts from his wrist crossbows at anyone who came at his group, putting one bolt in a soldier's throat and one into another's eye. Tempest walks into the middle of the city alone, leaving a path of rot and decay behind her and sees a group running down an alley. She follows, comes around the corner, and takes a mace to the side of her face and uses the force of the hit to spin her around and slam her lance into the person's stomach, sending him back and gets slashed at the back. She makes both wings slam together, catching the person in the rotting wings and causing them to rot from each part that got hit. Jake rode by on his motorcycle, slashing at Tempest and causing a cut across her.

Tempest thrust forward, hitting a soldier's shield and causing it to rust and knocking him on the ground. Before she could finish him off, she takes another shot from the guy on the motorcycle and takes flight only to fly into a guy jumping from the building, taking her to the ground and rotting. As soon as he hits her, she shoves him off, gets to her feet, and sees the motorcycle doing a wheelie straight into her face and driving her down, slamming her head into the ground and smashing he face in and going off her.

She gets back to her feet to everyone's amazement and launches her lance like a javelin at Jake, impaling him straight through the stomach and through his spine and taking him off his motorcycle before turning into a bunch of arrows from archers and falling dead to the ground.

Tindell: I said send guards first.

Guard captain: The attack sped that decision.

Werewolf: I think you have wandered into the wrong den.

Guard captain: Weapons are ready.

Werewolf: Do you not think one werewolf can take on six armed men?

Guard captain: We are just trying to travel through.

Werewolf: Well, are you the leader of this group?

Guard captain: Yes. We need some help.

Werewolf: I can take you to Vector.

Guard captain: Please do.

Vector: What do you want?

Guard captain: Just passing through. Maybe some help from you.

Vector: (*smirks*) You want help from a group that you shunned from the city and forced into the sewers? Why would I possibly want to help you at all?

Guard captain: We promise that after this war, we will treat you as equals, even allow you a spot on the council.

Vector: That will not be enough, but we can decide on the rest later. What did you need help with?

Guard captain: Just let the city through and maybe hold off our enemies.

Vector: And who are we fighting?

Guard captain: Stingers.

Vector: Never heard of them. Oh well.

Leech: The sewers. Great.

Acrid: Afraid of the dark.

Leech: I'm afraid of nothing. It smells like shit.

Acrid: It's the sewers where shit goes.

Vector: Those are stingers. Kill them. Don't hesitate at all.

Three werewolves take down two stingers and a rot angel and start tearing into them with teeth and claws, and before they know it, the two on stingers' claws and jaws start melting away. The one on the rot angel starts rotting away.

Vector: What is this deception from the humans again? I will kill them. Send a peace group to meet with the stingers group. With that, we will surely lose one for everyone we kill. We'd run out of men first. And send a group to kill the humans that betrayed us.

Acrid: Look! A werewolf under the sign of peace. I'm sure Inferno will be interested in this. Who are you?

Werewolf: Just a messenger. Vector wished to speak with your leader.

Acrid: Wait here. Leech want to get Inferno.

Leech: Why not? I love being a messenger with my high rank.

Inferno: Lead us on.

Inferno arrives in a large chamber along with Leech, Acrid, and many of Inferno's royal guards with Vector across from them, sitting on a throne.

Vector: Greetings, king of the stingers! (*bows before him*)

Inferno: You want to talk under a sign of peace even though you killed three of my men.

Vector: An unfortunate misunderstanding. We wish to join with you.

Inferno: Another big advantage can be reached with this.

Vector: And to prove it, I have a group hunting the refugees in the sewers.

Inferno: How about you let some digger stingers join you?

Vector: A digger?

Inferno: Yes. A type of stinger that has tail-like arms and a snakelike body that travels underground pretty easily that water will be the same around them.

Vector: At least I will see your men in action.

Mayor: How far until we get to the next town?

Guard Captain: Not far. Maybe a mile, but its hard to tell in this maze.

Ezekiel: I hear something. We're being followed.

Gabriel: Get the men ready.

After Ezekiel says that, he slammed to the ground with a digger who tries to impale Ezekiel's head. Ezekiel barely moves in time and stabs his assassin blade into the digger's eye, getting some acid blood on his cheek, which starts burning, and Ezekiel wipes it off, burning his hand, and throws the digger off. A digger stabs through a fighter's leg and pulls him into the water.

Guard: We have reinforce— (A werewolf tackles him to the ground and shreds the unfortunate guard's face.)

A werewolf goes after Gabriel and gets a slash across his stomach, getting four cuts and doing minor damage and goes for a throat slash. Gabriel ducks and has his short swords doing a double stab at the werewolf's torso, stabbing the wolf and pushing him into the water.

Gabriel thinks, *They don't know angels carry holy weapons— including silver.*

A big digger comes out of the water and tries to smash Gabriel. He sidesteps and slashes the arm, drawing a long gash across the arm. The digger pulls back, and Gabriel drops a sword and draws his .50-caliber handgun and unloads on the digger, putting half a clip into it before it falls.

Ezekiel was barely up before getting hit by a werewolf who slashes across Ezekiel's face, slicing his entire cheek through and tries to bite Ezekiel's throat. Ezekiel gets his sword up and pushes it through the werewolf's mouth, cutting its head in half. Ezekiel sidesteps a leaping digger and uses wind to blow it back into the werewolves. Another digger leaps out only to get a chop to the throat from a monk, breaking its throat, but before it dies, it stabs the monk with its biggest stinger, knocking him into the wall and leaving a gaping hole in his stomach with poison spreading fast. Knowing he's gonna die, he charges the first werewolf back up and hits it with a flying kick to its mouth, knocking some teeth out, He strikes its chest, breaking a rib before two more wolves take it to the ground, slashing him apart.

Gabriel shoots the remaining of his clip—which is about four shots—into the wolves, killing about eight. And then a wolf bigger than the others comes through and backhands Gabriel across the sewer into the wall, and Gabriel falls into the water where a digger bites onto him and pulls him under his gun, which is now gone. He stabs blindly at his attacker and knows he hit it as water gets hotter from the acid blood of the digger. He is released from the grip, and he rushes for the surface and pulls himself out, only see that by that time, that wolf has killed multiple people, and Ezekiel is having trouble handling it.

Ezekiel seems to be staying alive with a number of wounds. His right arm has some big gashes. He has a chunk taken out of his stomach. He's only managed a couple cuts on the big wolf's arms. Gabriel springs across the water and slashes the back of the wolf's knee and dives between its legs with a roll before another wolf gets him and slashes through the big wolf's groin and gets to his feet by Ezekiel. Ezekiel takes the distraction and stabs the big wolf's torso about a dozen times and jumps back from a slash and takes one of its fingers off and gets down as the crossbow men unload a flurry of arrows onto it. It drops, and the first ones over are dropped right away.

Guard: Come on. With the explosives set to close, the tunnel is behind us.

CHAPTER 12

Inferno: Welcome to my capital. This is where I rule my kingdom. This way.

Scientist: King Inferno, how may I serve you?

Inferno: I've made a new alliance and would like to see if your neutralizing effects work. That way, we can have a were-stinger.

Vector: I'm not biting any of your stingers.

Inferno: Send one of your men.

Inferno: So it's a success. We have created were-stingers.

Vector: All we made were abominations. These things are hideous. They don't even look like stingers or werewolves.

Inferno: Their appearances don't matter. All we did is make an even worse group of creatures that will help me take over.

Mayor: Is that the way out?

Guard captain: Yes. They make their way out.

City guard: Who are you?

Mayor: We are refugees from Carville. It's been attacked, and we're all that's left. We seek an audience with the mayor here.

Guard: Okay. We'll determine who you are. Until then, you will be taken into custody, and you can have a council with the mayor then.

Cosgove mayor: So you're supposed to be the Carville mayor. Well, what we can tell? Carville is burned, so your story fits. But how is it that from that town only about fifty people are alive.

Carville mayor: We were attacked by the stingers along with werewolves in the tunnels.

Cosgove mayor: Why would werewolves attack you?

Carville mayor: Because we shunned and exiled them to the sewers.

Cosgove mayor: Well, maybe you should accept them like we have with vampires. This is Saren, a very high-up vampire who sits on the ruling council.

Saren: Well, if the werewolves are attacking with them, I can get my vampires to help, with werewolves being our sworn enemies.

Carville mayor- Vector's group is down in the sewers.

Saren: Damn sewers! I won't be able to use my special ability, and it's a big shot. Like Vector, he isn't unknown to the vampires. If you'll excuse me, I have to get ready for this.

Ezekiel: Saren, do you want our help to deal with Vector?

Saren: No. My vampires and I will deal with this wolf ourselves. Let's go.

Vampire: This way is blocked by a cave.

Saren: We'll find a way around.

Vampire: There's another tunnel over here that leads around.

Saren: Let's go. Don't want them finding out we're here.

They come into a large chamber.

Vector: Well, if it ain't Saren, the legendary vampiric dragon in just his vampire form. Well, this will be fun. You can't transform in here, can you?

Saren: I won't need to kill you.

Vector: Oh, you're here to kill me. Maybe I should run away while you fight my men.

As his men surround the vampires, it looks like Vector and nine werewolves against me and nine vampires. Lucky break.

Vector charges for Saren, whips out his rapier, and goes for a straight stab for Vector's torso. Vector turns in time and takes it in the shoulder and slams Saren to the side. Saren gets back to his feet and readies for another attack from him and pulls out a small dagger and keeps it hidden. Vector goes for Saren again and gets stabbed in the stomach but didn't keep him.

He keeps moving forward, driving Saren down and bending Saren's blade to break in half. He lands on top of Saren and goes for Saren's throat, who blocks it with his arm. Vector swings his head to break Saren's arm and throws it out of the way, only to catch a knife in his eye. Vector yells and jumps back, getting the knife out of his eye. Saren jumps back to his feet. Vector rushes again and does a flip, twisting and landing on Vector's back and biting Vector's neck and stabbing him repeatedly in his side.

Vector falls backward, landing on Saren, and rolls off, going for some slashes and getting Saren's unbroken arm and a slash on the waist and lunges at Saren only to get his left bicep muscle sliced in half. Roaring in pain, Vector slashes at Saren, hits his torso, and breaks a few ribs and slices through the first two while taking another stab from Saren who—to Vector's surprise—can use fire breath in his vampire form, setting Vector ablaze.

Vector, knowing that the battle is going to end with him dead, decides to do as much damage. He pounces on Saren and immediately gets stabbed in the throat and face and starts slashing Saren until Saren stabs the dagger into the brain and Vector falls on Saren who pushes the now dead Vector off. He gets up to see that he only lost about half his group, and here's a sound from another tunnel. The most hideous thing Saren has ever seen emerged looks like a werewolf with horns, red eyes, teeth that looks to big for its mouth, ravenlike wings (has two instead of one tail, which have a scorpionlike tail on it), and its black fur with a bunch of tribal-like lines going across its fur.

Saren: What the fuck is that?

The were-stinger rushes forward and impales on the vampire through the neck and kicks Saren in the chest. Saren notices three sharper ends on its feet, shoves two other vampires away, grabs the third, bites down on his neck, and rips his throat out and head-butts him, driving his horns about a foot into his head and killing the vampire. The other two vampires with swords in hands start circling the were-stinger and attack at the same time. The were-stinger's tails parry the first vampire's strike.

The were-stinger kicks the vampire in front with the bottom of his foot, driving his foot on top of the vampire and breaking his rib cage. It opens its hand and aims at the vampire, and a dark ball appears and shoots at the vampire's face, blowing the vampire's head apart. The were-stingers' two tails impale the other vampire through the gut and ribs. The were-stinger grabs the vampire's head and rips it off, turns to look at Saren, and launches a fireball at him, which he dodges. The were-stinger anticipated this and meets him, kneeing him under the chin and sending Saren up before grabbing his head and slamming him into the ground, then takes and throws him into a wall.

Saren: I'm not a natural dragon. I've learned multiple types of breath. Let's see if you can take ice.

Saren launches an ice breath at the were-stinger that stops it with flames and ends up trying to overpower the others. The were-stinger starts walking forward where he and Saren are only a foot apart. Saren stabs forward with his knife into his chest. The were-stinger tries, head-butting into Saren's head who backs up only grazing him but able to stop his breath, taking some scorching half his face. The were-stinger slams his hand into Saren's gut and starts pulling out his intestines. Saren starts stabbing him in the face and hits him with a lightning breath, blasting him into a wall and breaking the were-stinger's neck. Saren collapses to his knees and coughs up some blood.

Saren: What the fuck was that? Heard something from the tunnel. Looks at it out come three more were stingers.

Saren thinks, *I may be in a sewer, but I'm gonna need to go dragon from a smash out of here.*

Saren changes into a big red dragon, slams through the ceiling, and fire breaths the chamber, turning into a scorching inferno and forcing the were-stingers back down the tunnel. Saren retreats back to the town.

Days fast approaching. Good thing I'm a day walker.

CHAPTER 13

Inferno: What a pretty face you have, Reva. I decided that you will become a member of my army. I will bound you by spell, and I will transform you into a tainted blood, but you will be transformed with the blood of the king—me.

Inferno takes Reva forward, puts a syringe filled with poison and one with his blood in her neck, and injects it. The guards let Reva go, and she hits the ground and starts convulsing.

Inferno: When she's done with that, take her to her new room. Until then, I will cast a spell on her. If she turns on me or anyone under me, she will die a painful death.

Ezekiel: It's time we end this. These are the blueprints for Inferno's place and a secret way in, thanks to Raptor. We'll remember him, but when we get in, we need to kill Inferno and his main generals. With them all dead, they will just scatter, and his ranks and kingdom will fall apart.

Saren: They have created new abominations. I say not to stop there. We should kill all of them. This should be a full-scale genocide on the stingers to make sure this does not happen again.

Ezekiel: This is a war. This is not to kill off an entire species. We can't judge them over what their tyrant leader does.

Saren: Well, my vampires and I will kill as much as possible. You can take your troops and do what you want. That's what I'm going to do.

Ezekiel: Saren, we need you with the infiltration team.

Saren: I hope you know I'll kill every stinger I come across.

Ezekiel: Fine. We'll be in Inferno's castle. That will be accepltibly. So what's the plan?

Ezekiel: We'll have an army attack at Inferno's main capital, then while they are distracted with that, we will infiltrate Inferno's castle, find his throne room, and kill him and his main men. We will begin traveling in the hour. Get all equipment ready.

Acrid: Inferno, we have an army approaching.

Inferno: Really?

Acrid: Yes. Looks like they are trying to end the war.

Inferno: Get the army ready. Get the werewolves, demon stingers, and were-stingers, and destroy the enemy army.

Lone Wolf: My lord.

Inferno: What is it?

Lone Wolf: The army is just a distraction.

Inferno: What do you mean?

Lone Wolf: We have a small—seems to be about three men— sneaking in. Looks like they want to assassinate you.

Inferno: Go bring Stryke, Kestix, Reva, and Rickter here. Take my royal guard, the shifer, and Acrid, and I want the three of you to kill them.

Lone Wolf: Yes, sir.

Lone Wolf: Well, if it isn't the legendary warriors—the vampire dragon, Saren; the fallen angel, Ezekiel; and his friend, Gabriel. Your trick and life ends here.

Ezekiel: I'll take the rot angel. Gabriel, I want you to take the shadow stinger, and Saren, take on the last one.

Acrid launches some rot bolts from his wrist crossbow at Ezekiel who dodges and blocks one and goes at Acrid with his assassin blade and is blocked. Acrid's rot assassin blade and starts rusting Ezekiel's weapon. Acrid swings his claw at Ezekiel's head. Ezekiel goes under and thrusts his short sword forward into Acrid's armor, and it just dents it. Acrid flies up and launches about fifteen rot bolts down on Ezekiel.

He rolls forward and draws a knife that he throws up at Acrid, hitting him in the exposed wing and lands a few feet away, and Ezekiel slashes his sword downward at Acrid's exposed wing, cutting it off. Acrid slashes his claw at Ezekiel's face, barely nicking Ezekiel's remaining one ear. Ezekiel goes with his assassin blade for Acrid's neck. Acrid grabs Ezekiel's gaunlenent and spits into Ezekiel's face, and his face starts to burn. Ezekiel uses magic to blow it off.

Acrid suddenly goes into a flurry of shots, putting Ezekiel on the defensive, and Acrid grabs Ezekiel around the throat, and Ezekiel has a hard time breathing while his skin on his throat starts turning black. Before Ezekiel notices that Acrid's hand has no armor, he cuts his hand off, then goes for Acrid's throat. As he stumbles back, Acrid gets his remaining hand up, but the blade goes right through his hand, but he keeps the blade away. Ezekiel brings his short sword around, stabbing it into the side of Acrid's head and out the other and then yanks the sword up, coming out of Acrid's head and killing him.

Acrid's rotting blood starts flowing out of the wound. Gabriel starts slashing and thrusting at Lone Wolf with his short sword, keeping Lone Wolf from getting in with his daggers, but then Lone Wolf surprises Gabriel by rushing forward, cutting a gash across Gabriel's chest, a gash across his forearm, and a jagged cut on his forehead. He rolls back, and Gabriel is amazed at the precision and speed that Lone Wolf has with his daggers. Gabriel slashes low, and Lone Wolf jumps over and rushes in, stabbing a dagger deep into Gabriel's shoulder. Gabriel slams the hilt of one of his swords into Lone Wolf's face. Lone Wolf takes the shot and does a back handstand and lands on his feet but lost one dagger in the process. Still on Gabriel's shoulder, Gabriel pulls it out and throws it on the ground.

Lone Wolf: I thought you were a better fighter that that.

Gabriel is angered and attacks quick and fast. Lone Wolf slashes his dagger through the side of Gabriel's gut and slides past to grab his second dagger.

Lone Wolf: So easily tricked and angered. How sad. Thought you would know better.

Gabriel cautiously walks forward, watching Lone Wolf for a weakness. Lone Wolf lunges forward and slashes Gabriel's cheek, his nose, the side of his neck, and puts a cut on his thigh, then rolls to the right. And Gabriel realizes it—Lone Wolf rushes forward each time. Lone Wolf goes forward again, but Gabriel gets his blades positioned to impale Lone Wolf on them, then releases one of them, grabs his gun, and aims at Lone Wolf's face. He pulls the trigger, blowing his head to bits, and retrieves his sword.

Saren draws his new rapier, and the shifter goes into an unarmed fighting stance. Saren goes for a thrust. The shifter knocks the rapier away, then punches Saren in the face. Saren staggers back and feels the three cuts across his face. The stinger's arm turns into a studded mace then it hits Saren in the chest, breaking a few ribs. Saren is looking down due to the hit, and the stinger's foot changed into the head of a sledge arm and kicks him in the face, shattering his nose.

Saren, stabbing at the stinger's gut and drawing only a little blood, then backs quickly as a wicked-looking blade barely nicks Saren's neck, and then the stinger's dreadlocks turn into what appears to be cobras, and these spit at him. Saren dodges it and notices that where it hit, it starts sizzling, meaning that it's acid, and his fingers turn to blades and slashes at Saren, which Saren dodges back from going for another stab at his eye. He grabs the blade and twists it to break Saren's wrist.

Saren blasts the stinger with his ice breath, freezing it. Just as Gabriel and Ezekiel finish with their fight, Gabriel then shoots the ice form, destroying the frozen stinger. They then rush through the castle, trying to find the throne room. They find it with no more residents.

Inferno: Hello! Well, isn't this a fitting battle? If you lose, I win, but there's no chance of you beating me. Oh and Ezekiel, you may be a little happy. Your daughter Reva is here, but not only that. She's taken my blood, turning her into a tainted blood stinger.

Reva: Sorry, Father, but I can't resist him. One of you must kill me. I'm not your sweet little daughter. I'm your enemy. If you hesitate at all, I will kill you.

Stryke: Angel, we will join you in this.

Inferno: betrayed I will enjoy killing you as well.

Reva launches a thunderbolt at Ezekiel, but he dodges to the side.

Ezekiel: Resist it! When this ends, we can go back to living the way we did before. We'll go to your mom's funeral.

Reva: I'll send you to her.

Reva launches a fireball at Ezekiel. He rolls under it and burns his back. Reva launches an ice spike at Ezekiel, hitting him in the ribs. He ignores the pain, slamming his assassin blade into Reva's gut and pulling her forward. He tells her he's sorry and cuts Reva's head off.

Gabriel turns to take on Rickter who swings at his legs with vengeance. Gabriel jumps over the chain, and he uses his wings to fly forward. Rickter swings his chain upward, hitting Gabriel in his groin and wrapping up over his shoulder. Rickter pulls Gabriel into the ground and then shortens the length, dragging Gabriel to Rickter who then swings his sword down at Gabriel's head who barely moves his head and flies up, dragging Rickter up as well and flying up to the chandelier.

Rickter lets go of the chain and is caught by Emerald. Gabriel turns back and flies back at them, and Emerald throws earth spikes in front of Gabriel who stops it, gets his feet on it, propels himself up, and dive-bombs at Rickter, cutting through his arm and rendering it useless. Rickter grabs a light cylinder from his pocket and throws it at the ground, creating a flashing light and blinding Gabriel.

Rickter and Emerald use that time to get out of the throne room and get away. Kestix attacks Midnight, swinging his scythe at Midnight who jumps over the scythe and slashes at Kestix's gut, cutting three lines across him. Midnight sends his two poison tails at Kestix who swings his scythe, cutting off Midnight's two tails. He bites down on Kestix's arm, breaking his arm and twisting around, trying to rip his arm off. Kestix slams the handle on Midnight's head, lets the scythe go, and gouges out two of Midnight's eyes, forcing Midnight to let go and kicking Midnight in the jaw, lifting off the ground. Kestix elbows him in the head, and Midnight jumps at Kestix who slides forward, angling his scythe up. Midnight's speed carries Midnight through the blade, cutting him in half.

Leech rushes at Stryke and swings his hammer to the side. Stryke blocks it with his spiked shield, breaking a spike off and denting it, then Leech backhands with the axe side, hitting the side of the shield and cutting into it. Leech does an upward slash with the hook, pulling it out of the way and slamming the hammer into Stryke's head, breaking half of Stryke's skull and sending him across the room and seeing Kestix kill Midnight, who then turns around after getting hit by an upward slash from Leech's hook.

Saren transforms into a big red dragon, then looks down on Inferno who draws his flamberge. Saren blows his fire breath at Inferno who positions his flamberge in front of him, and the fire starts being consumed into the flamberge.

Inferno: Surprised? Saren, my flamberge is powered by flames, and you just fed it a lot of power. Let me show you what I mean.

Inferno points his flamberge at Saren, and it launches a gigantic fireball at Saren, exploding on the side of his head. Saren's scales turn black, and Saren hits him. Inferno just stands and lets it hit him, and his armor starts corroding, but Inferno just laughs.

Inferno: Hahaha. Did you forget that since stingers have an acidic blood, we have a natural immunity to acid?

Saren now turns to a blue dragon and hits Inferno with ice breath, freezing him.

Saren: You're not immune to everything.

And then the ice just shatters, going different directions. Saren covers his exposed eyes with a wing, and when he uncovers it, Inferno is no longer frozen.

Inferno: Did you really think that would beat me?

Saren turns black and launches a poison gas at Inferno who just launches a fireball into it, causing an explosion leading back to Saren's face. Saren's head snaps back. Inferno rushes forward and leaps into the air and flies at Saren's face, cutting off a horn and scorching the horn, then launching a dark stinger blast at Saren's other horn, disintegrating it. Now blood is running down where Saren's horn was just at.

Saren tries to snap his jaws on Inferno who just jumps to the side and brings his flamberge down on Saren's nose, taking a scale off and making a small cut and burning the skin, opening the wound even more. Saren slams his claws down on Inferno who only catches it and lifts Saren into the air, then slams him on the ground and lands a series of slashes and thrusts on Saren's stomach, causing intense pain on Saren who turns into a white dragon.

He hits Inferno with lightning breath, sending Inferno into a wall. Inferno stands back up as Saren goes for more lightning breath, and Inferno catches it with his flamberge, directing it back at Saren who can't dodge in time, shocking Saren and burning some of his organs. Saren collapses in front of Inferno who just picks Saren up and throws him through the giant window behind his throne and sends six dark stinger blasts after each, exploding one after the other. Inferno watches Saren's dragons drop to the valley, then turns to see the battle in his throne room.

Leech notices Ezekiel leaning over his dead daughter. He then thinks, *This is a perfect time to kill the fallen angel.* Leech walks toward him.

Gabriel notices this and runs toward them. Leech sends his axe side toward Ezekiel's neck. Gabriel jumps, knocking Ezekiel out of the way but taking the axe through his back and out the other side. Ezekiel stands up.

Ezekiel: I'm going to kill you! You're the one that killed my wife, responsible for my daughter having to die, and you killed my best friend. I don't care about defeating Inferno as long as I can kill you.

Ezekiel angrily attacks Leech, putting him on the defensive but—with his smaller, quicker weapons—gets a lot of strikes through, denting and scratching Leech's armor. He backs Leech near the end of the window. Inferno sees a chance. He then launches a dark stinger blast at both Ezekiel and Leech. Both notice, and Ezekiel jumps back, but Leech isn't fast enough. The blast hits Leech and explodes, sending Leech out of the castle and down the long drop. The explosion's shock wave hits Ezekiel, sending him across the room.

Ezekiel: You killed Leech, robbing me of my vengeance.

Inferno: It was meant to end like this—me against you. You did well. My generals are dead, but that's only a delay. I will overcome.

Ezekiel, still filled with rage, attacks Inferno relentlessly that Inferno fends off easily and steps the last slash. Ezekiel steps forward off balance Inferno pummel strikes Ezekiel in the back of the head. Stryke notices what's going on, runs at Inferno, and shield bashes Inferno, breaking Inferno's damaged chest plate. Stryke goes for a high slash. Inferno drops below and swings at Stryke who blocks with his shield, but the strike staggers him back and numbs his arm, then Inferno hits another strike.

Stryke trips over part of Midnight's dead body. Inferno just hammers away at Stryke's shield. Kestix rushes at Inferno. They then trade blows—Kestix's big scythe against Infernos giant flamberge. Inferno gets his flamberge against Kestix's scythe and turns, grabbing stomach and throwing him over onto Kestix's back and stomping down on Kestix's throat.

Ezekiel stabs Inferno in the back with his assassin's blade. Inferno elbows Ezekiel in the gut, knocking him back and gets a slash across the back from Stryke's long sword. Inferno goes for a slash at Stryke. Ezekiel rushes in and stabs Inferno under the arm.

Inferno turns back to get Ezekiel, and Stryke slashes at Inferno's leg, cutting it behind the knee and taking him to one knee. Inferno drops his flamberge and fireballs Stryke who blocks with his shield a dark demon blast. Ezekiel dodges it. Kestix gets onto his knees and notices the chandelier above Inferno, then throws his scythe with all his strength at it, cutting the chain and sending it falling, landing on Inferno with the sharpened point smashing into his head and crushing below it.

Ezekiel: Thanks for the help. Guess not all stingers are bad.

Stryke: Not all. Inferno was an evil tyrant. I'm glad we stopped him. Let us get the Wolf Pack, and we will help clear out his army.

Ezekiel: No then attacking got strict orders to kill every stinger. I think you and your squad should hide and return when things aren't as bad for your species. Might take half a century, but I know you guys don't die of old age.

Stryke: Maybe we'll meet again someday.

Ezekiel: I hope so.

Kestix: Well, this isn't the ending I expected for killing Inferno.

Ezekiel: I'm sorry, but I'm not in control. Saren ordered the vampires, and the humans agreed. Most of my company is dead.

Stryke: Okay. Kestix, get the members. We will go into hiding. Search us out if you need help. We're no longer the Wolf Pack. Inferno gave us that name. We will now be known as the Renegade Squad.

Saren: (*gets up*) I can't believe I survived that.

He then flies back toward the castle, enters, and notices that Inferno is dead.

Ezekiel: Oh, Saren, maybe you can help me carry my daughter and Gabriel out of here. They deserve a proper funeral, but we need to raise a new flag.

The vampiric and human alliance flag is risen, then the demons and werewolves turn on the stingers, killing a big number of them badly. Hardly any got away. But then the demons started fighting against the humans, and in the confusion, some stingers got away. Leech survived the fall and explosion and finds a little group of stingers fleeing, including Inferno's pregnant wife, Tehila.

Leech: I'm sorry, but Inferno must have died.

Tehila: Well, if his kid is a boy, I will name him Blaze in honor of his father.

Ezekiel: You guys want to erase all history of the stingers.

Saren: Yes. They can make new stingers by turning them into tainted blood, so we want to erase them so they don't come back.

And that is story of the great Stinger war, and that's how my grandfather died.
—Riken